THE SEARCH FOR INFINITY
© 2015 Alina Ben Larbi

Die Deutsche Nationalbibliothek verzeichnet diese Publikation in der Deutschen Nationalbibliografie; detaillierte bibliografische Daten sind im Internet unter www.dnb.de abrufbar.

Mit Fotografien der Autorin
Translation: Euan Robertson
Herstellung und Verlag: BoD – Books on Demand, Norderstedt
ISBN 9-783752-824254

The Search for Infinity

by Alina Ben Larbi

When little Paula had witnessed her 14th moon, she learned of an intangibly unimaginable creature. No one had ever seen it or really knew anything about it. Only myths made mention of it. At first, Paula was afraid of the beast and fervently hoped that this monster would never get anywhere near her. However, her pity for this legendary animal - which was feared and ridiculed by all - grew more and more. For an entire moon she thought about whether there could really be something so terrible in this dimension, and whether it was actually a very lovable something, a very loveable something that unfortunately had become a victim of mischaracterisation by so many. It probably sat in a dark room and cried miserably because it had no friends.

When Paula asked her father (who always knew everything) after a few stars, he simply replied: "Don't worry about it! It's a waste of time, as nobody will ever find out what this being truly is and whether it even exists or not."

Paula was disappointed, as she had once dreamed of finding the creature and stroking it. Now her clever father claimed that it might not even exist at all. At that moment, she doubted whether he really was that clever. If he was, he surely wouldn't settle for mere ignorance.

So, before the sun disappeared behind the seventh planet, she asked her mother if the creature had a name. Her answer only consisted of four words, the last of which would captivate Paula for the longest of times. "Its name is Infinity." said her mother.

After Paula repeated the word quietly, she asked: "How can it have a name if it has no one to say its name?" As she often was, Paula's mother became overwhelmed and, as she often did when she was overwhelmed, she said: "Do your homework!"

That day Paula had nothing to do, and after sitting in her room for a short while, she looked outside and decided to find out what this mysterious Infinity was really all about.

Firstly, she went to her grandmother. She had lived for 578 moons and had white hair, so she had to know more than her "clever" son. After her grandmother made a hot chocolate for Paula - and promptly added a few marshmallows - Paula started her interview.

"Grandma, what is Infinity, and where can I find it?"

As much as she had hoped, she had been expecting a similar response to what she had received from her teachers and parents. That is why the reaction of her beloved father's mother came as a surprise.

"Infinity is not a place, an object, or even a living being. You can look for it, but you won't get there or find it. A life is long, but an infinity is longer. It is the longest thread in the sewing box we call the World. It is the thread that has no beginning and no end, and yet it does not form a clear circle. It is a contradiction of terms, where an error cannot be found. It's insane to solve, so put that idea out of your mind. Only when you are no longer distracted from all the thinking can you start seeing without your eyes.

You will find the answer, but you will not recognize it. It lies in colourful paintings on the walls of your mind. But you will not understand them, for your mind is no longer given to you on a silver platter. Reel it back in and the paintings disappear. Let it float away, and you wander around like a blind man who knows colours. Infinity will watch you with a smile. We're its playthings, and she's hiding alongside us. We are the Seekers, yet it is always infinitely ahead of us."

Paula was mature for her age, but such complicated statements overwhelmed her for the time being. After thinking for a few seconds, she said: "You speak in riddles. Is the answer to this riddle that I will never find Infinity?"

"I'm afraid so." was her grandmother's response.

But Paula wouldn't give up that easily.

After the twelfth planet had passed the sun once more, she set off to see her best friend, Jacob. He was the smartest student in her class and was always open to hearing new ideas and giving wise advice. On this star, Paula had seen him speechless for the first time in her life when she asked him about Infinity.

"I don't know," he confessed, "because I've never seen it myself. Those stories that say it's evil? I don't want to believe them. I think it's only feared because it's unknown. People are always afraid of the unknown. They seek security in a safe world, but they will never find it if they imagine all uncertainty as evil."

Jacob had given a good answer. Even though he hadn't given Paula the solution she was looking for, he had helped her to be brave and move on in the world to solve this mystery.

She packed her bags full of her favourite cookies and left. She passed the strangest people, asking them all about Infinity, only to be made fun of when she added that she was looking for it.

After seventeen stars she came to a city that consisted entirely of numbers. The houses were built from numbers, the ground was entirely made of them, and even the clothes of the people around her. Paula was tired from running and finally knocked on a door that seemed to have been carved from a three. She heard it echo throughout the house and wondered whether she should instead sleep under the open moon. Just as she had decided to leave again, a figure opened and stood in the doorway. He wore a brown cloak made of numbers with so many decimal places she couldn't count them.

"Yes?" the figure barked in an unfriendly manner. "Sorry to bother you, but I would like to ask for your help. "I need a place to rest on my long journey towards Infinity."

Paula did not expect a polite answer, let alone that she would be let in, but the figure opened the door a little further and hurriedly replied: "Come in, quickly!".   He looked around outside once more and then followed Paula back into the house. Here too everything was carved out of numbers, but Paula often seemed to find the number three. "If I may introduce myself, my name is Zacharias. Tsar of the number city and number gnome," said the figure. "Paula," Paula replied, wondering how she could add more prestige to her presence. After all, her counterpart was a tsar of an entire city, and she could merely give her name. "How do you do?"

Zacharias then interrupted the ensuing silence. "So, Paula, tell me how a little girl like you wants to find Infinity so badly?"

"Curiosity is what allows me to survive this search. Do you know anything about Infinity?"

"I'd be lying if I replied with a resounding 'yes'." confessed the number gnome. "But I *can* tell you the secret of our town if you promise to keep it to yourself."

Paula promised high and holy not to tell anyone, so he went on. "Well, it is..." he began his speech. "We residents of Numbers City are passionate number collectors, but such a passion is not as easy as you might think. You can't just go into a shop and buy some numbers, you have to earn them. A 5 is easy to get, but what about a 572,183,389? Even the elders of our city will never be able to produce a complete collection... because nobody knows how to own one. For many generations we have been trying to compile an entire numerological collection, but it seems as if we have been busy with it for an eternity. Our reputation in other cities would be tarnished if they knew about such an insurmountable problem."

"Why must it be unsolvable? I think you just have to think about it some more," said Paula, and was instantly afraid of offending the number gnome. Zacharias looked at Paula with great interest and asked if she had a solution. Although the sun was already covered by ten planets, Paula and the Tsar went outside. They passed many numbers, but none of them took to Paula's liking until she stopped in front of town's big church clock and pointed up its stairs. "We have to go up there," she ordered.

The Tsar was not accustomed to carrying out orders, but he obeyed and followed Paula up the long spiral staircase in the tower anyway. There, Paula stood in front of the large clockface and reached to for the eight to take into her hand. She then gave it to the number gnome. "Here's your complete collection," she stated, but he didn't understand. "All you have to do is put this number on its side and you'll have everything you need."

Zacharias was speechless. Every inhabitant of the city of numbers had tired countless moons thinking about how to finish the collection and now a little girl comes and solves the ancient riddle.

Even on the next star, when Paula had already slept in and set off, he continued to look speechlessly at the small infinity in his hand.

Our heroine was incredibly proud to have freed a city from its worries and walked on until she could no longer see the city of numbers. However, her good mood was momentarily clouded by a new thought. Had she now *also* finished her search by solving the problem of the city of numbers? After all, she had given Zacharias an infinity. Could you just turn a number and solve the puzzle? The more she thought about it, the less she liked the idea that her search was ended by a 90° turn. At some point she came to the conclusion that finding something was not the only factor in finding something. If she was looking for Jacob and wrote his name on a piece of paper, she would not have found him either. Satisfied with this realization, she now continued her journey with renewed anticipation.

She met many astonished and annoyed faces on the next stretch of her route, but she did not let them stop her. If someone was unkind to her, she didn't have to stay with them. Nevertheless, it was an immense pity that our little Paula met with so much rejection. Few offered their food or a place to sleep, for most thought it was outrageous that such an inquisitive young girl wandered the world alone, claiming that she was looking for Infinity. Little by little Paula became sad and got even a bit homesick. No one wanted to greet her with kindness. When she used to walk back home, she thought of her family and friends there, people who she could laugh with. She considered to just turning around and going home for a while, but couldn't keep her curiosity at bay.

After a long star, when nine planets already kept the sunlight away, her way was blocked by a large lake. She knew it would take a long time to bypass or cross it, so she wanted to spend the night on its shore to sleep until the nearest star and continue the journey post-haste.

However, she did not find a suitable place to sleep very quickly, and ran around for a while until her search was interrupted by the warmest of feelings. The sadness she had felt was diminishing. Every piece of space left behind by her - now dwindling - sadness was filled with a new, yet familiar feeling. She was so surprised by this that she stopped and enjoyed it as she slowly took in this strange joy, like a dried sponge absorbing emotions. She stayed there for almost a tenth of a star and eagerly hoped that this condition would last for many more tenths of a star.

However, it was interrupted by a new acquaintance, for the feeling did not come by chance. The cause was a source of both smiles and tears. Paula had stumbled across a love nymph.

"Love nymphs belong, as their name surely suggests, to the genus: nymph. They are nature spirits and thus have a mystical connection to the smaller parts of the natural world, such as a plant, a body of water, or on rare occasions, even a living being. Love nymphs, on the other hand, are the embodiment of the connection between the creatures. When the organism to which a nymph is bound dies, the same fate awaits the nymph itself. In the case of the Love Nymph, this means that she would die if there was no love left in the world. Like others of her kind, she cares for harmony on both sides of the connection. So, she simultaneously gives and gains love, because love grows when it is shared."

The nymph Paula met on her journey was named Natalia and had been sitting in a tree by the lake for thirty-seven stars, but not because she enjoyed it. One of her many sisters, a tree nymph, had made Natalia guard her tree for a short while. Since the other nymph did not return and Natalia was a loyal soul, she sat there, star after star on the shore waiting for her sister to return. So it was that Paula became part of the nymph's life's work.

The young tree keeper had felt Paula's presence as soon as she approached her and was immediately pleased that after such a long time she had found someone with whom she could share her love. She was briefly tempted by the thought of getting up and going over to Paula, but she did not want to abandon the tree and her sister. So, she stayed where she was and tried to choose the words that would scare Paula the least. Paula was stunned by the nymph's invitation to come see her, and with each step in her direction her heart became more comforting. At last, she sat next to Natalia and was almost blinded by the aura that surrounded her.

"I'm so happy to have finally met a single soul! My name is Natalia. How did you get here? For half an eternity I haven't met any living creatures besides passing birds and a few small aquatic animals," the beautiful figure began the conversation. "My name is Paula, and I heard of Infinity half a moon ago. Now I'm looking for it. Can you tell me how to find it?"

Natalia laughed. *Of course* she could. After all, she was an expert on Infinity, indirectly.

"Have you ever heard of love nymphs, Paula? I'm one of those creatures. My job is to spread love. Love grows stronger when you share it, you know? So the more I give, the more there is for me and others. Love is the only infinite thing worth living for."

Paula was more than surprised, but she was happier to have finally found someone to let her in on the secrets she craved. She had found a teacher.

In the next stars, Natalia taught our little heroine all about love and its infinite value, infinite greatness, and infinite power. Paula understood everything very quickly, knowing the subject in a few stars almost as well as any love nymph.

She would have liked to learn much more, but her lessons were finished by the arrival of Natalia's sister. After leaving Natalia alone for so long, she returned to her tree to take it back. Natalia herself was sad that she had to leave Paula now, but knew she had to accomplish her mission in a place where there were more souls who could give and receive love.

Before she left, she said to Paula:

"Never forget how important it is to love! Every being shows love in its own way. So, if you can't see love, try to find some rose-tinted glasses in yourself and take a closer look at your surroundings. You will see that love can be found everywhere, because it is the only thing that will last and grow forever. It is the only thing that exists in infinite forms."

Touched by the words but sad about the farewell, Paula thought about her future. She knew that Natalia said that love was the only infinite thing. Yet, if there were infinite forms of love, why could there not be infinite forms of infinity? So, Paula picked up a few branches and built a small raft, because she finally wanted to discover more infinity. She then let herself be driven towards her destiny on the large lake.

Paula sat there waiting for a long time, yet she was always so full of anticipation for the infinity she would discover. Maybe she could find one she could see or touch? Or perhaps it would be difficult to find another infinity. Doubt washed over her at that moment, like the waves around her raft, which seemed to get bigger and bigger. At some point Paula had to hold on tight so as not to fall into the dark depths below.

The blue of the sky was replaced by an ever deeper grey until a drop of rain fell on her nose. As expected, it wasn't just a drop, and soon the water fell down like an avalanche from the air above our brave heroine and the lake around her. Even lightning lit up the sky from time to time, until the whole ordeal came together in a full-blown thunderstorm. Paula was scared. She had never been afraid of thunder and lightning, but here on the water everything was so different. Her raft threatened to capsize and she became ever colder as more and more water covered her dress. She hoped it would pass soon, but then a soft voice interrupted her thoughts.

"Where did you get the idea of taking such a tiny raft into such a large lake?" Paula was startled, almost falling into the water, but she caught herself before she did. Whoever or whatever just spoke was right. It was a bad idea. Yet, she tried to justify herself. "I just wanted to find Infinity, and it's faster to go over the lake than it is to go around it. But now I regret choosing the faster route."

"The infinite, you say? You speak to her now."

Speechless, Paula looked around. She saw nothing but water. Was infinity invisible? Was there only one true infinity? Was it possible the voice lied to her? So many questions went through Paula's head. "What do you mean?" was the one she chose to ask.

"What could be more infinite than the cycle? Nothing comes to mind. It always starts over, without beginning and without end," was the answer the voice gave.

"You're a cycle?", Paula chose as her next question.

"I'm *part* of the cycle. Oh, I didn't introduce myself. I am the spirit of the water. I'm sure we've met before, because where there's water, there's me. So you could say I rule this planet. Though, few people appreciate that fact."

Impressed by the words of the Water Spirit, Paula sat down on the floor of her little vessel and felt a sudden sense of safety. She knew nothing that surrounded her wanted her to end. She knew she had an ending. She longed for a life like that of water.

"I'd like to be like you. You have nothing to fear for. So you have nothing to fear," she sighed.

"But that's what I fear. The world around me consists of many ends that I have to watch star by star. The fear of those who expect an end is what I find most terrible. They know that their time is limited, but they live as if they were immortal. Nobody ever thanked me for extending, beautifying, and sustaining their time. Hardly anyone seems to know the true value of water."

With these words Paula understood that the love nymph was not quite right. Love was important, but so was water. Life was a balance of natural matter and the supernatural; for this knowledge she thanked the spirit of the water. As long as the storm raged, he told her about other places and other beings and about water, or as she called it: "The Essence of Life". Paula understood how rain and rivers came into being, but in much more detail than she had learned at school. Eventually the storm and rain settled until the spirit - and its attention - left Paula. Again, she felt lonely, but she thought of Natalia's words, which immediately gave her courage. However, the sight of the nearby shore lifted her spirits even higher.

So Paula continued on into her uncertain future with both a good mood and a feeling of joy. Yet, it would soon darken again, like the sky did during the last storm. She was supposed to find someone who would give her knowledge, but before she could do that she came across a creature that was the subject of sagas similar to those of lurch elves. After arriving at the shore, she ran along for a while. She rested next to a big tree in a small abandoned village.

She had only just fallen asleep when she heard a strange sound. It was a rustling from the leaves that brought her back from her sleep. She thought of birds and horse chestnuts, but certainly not of what the sound really was. Following the rustling Paula heard a crackling, and immediately afterwards a big *something* fell out from the top of the tree. Even after rubbing her eyes twice, she couldn't believe it. In front of her lay a fantastical Fantadu. The creature itself also seemed puzzled at its failed attempt at an entrance, and so they both spent a few dwarf planets looking at each other and processing the shock.

Once they had both recovered, the Fantadu said, "I don't know who you are and why you are, but I'm fine with you being with me."

Paula was sure she should say something, but she didn't know what, so she started simply by introducing herself. "I don't know why I am either."

"But you can choose that. Invent that. Think of that. I am every star because of something else."

"Then I am because I fell from a tree in the moon of 4738," Paula replied.

Now she was confused. She had barely spoken three sentences to her opponent and was no longer sure who she was. It was confusing and maddening.

"Unfortunately, the tales of fantastical Fantadus were mostly negative. It was said that if you were in contact with them for a long time, you could no longer distinguish between dimensions and no longer know who and where you were. They were told that they were crazy and thus dragged others into their madness. They themselves, on the other hand, could deal with said madness, while their victims increasingly surrendered to the infinite worlds of thought and gradually dissolved into reality. Because imagination was so boundless, so was the eccentricity of Fantadus."

For little Paula was both lucky and unlucky at the same time, for she had found an infinity, but also a sure way to the end.

She listened for a long time to the imaginary stories of the Fantadu, who told her about new worlds, strange beings and false facts. She just sat there, whilst her own thoughts dissolved ever more and were replaced by those of the Fantadu. She hadn't known her name for a long time and had completely forgotten what she was doing in this place. Her consciousness had clung on to the stories she was hearing and was now flying higher than the fifth planet. It crossed worlds that seemed beyond imagination and came to corners that could only be reached by the mind of a madman. It expanded and spread everywhere, even in things that were only possible with the infinity of the imagination. The Fantadu could have told Paula anything, and she would have recognized it as truth. Without realizing it, she became a silent puppet of the fantastical.

The hope that the disaster would have an end was not entirely unfounded. Actually, the victims of a fantastical Fantadu came to an end within infinity, but our Paula was very lucky that at the time of her internal captivity, external salvation was fast approaching.

Professor Prudens Astrum - currently considered the most intelligent life form on the planet - was in the middle of research for invisible wings when he saw little Paula lying on a tree with her eyes glazed over. As the smartest person in the world at that time, he could tell by her eyes alone that she had fallen into the clutches of a fantasy Fantadu. He promptly dropped his tools, picked Paula up in his arms, and brought her as carefully as he could to his research station.

He knew that it would take a long time to awaken her from the Fantadu-induced dream, but he also knew that he should not only collect, but also share and use his knowledge.

So, he began to gather as many of his books about the world and the universe (most of which he had written himself) as possible. Word for word, line for line, chapter for chapter, book for book, he worked his way through the stack reading aloud for Paula. She lay on a small bed and listened to the words of the renowned professor until she finally remembered her body and name once more.

She slowly awakened from her paralysis, until the books finally ran out and she was again the old, clever, inquisitive, and above all – courageous, Paula. Now she was able to address her savior for the first time: "I don't know how to thank you. You saved my life. My happiness was restored by your kindness. My name is Paula, by the way. I came from far away to find Infinity."

"Good to see you alive, Paula! I'm Professor Prudens Astrum. If it's true that you're looking for infinity, then you've surely already come up with the idea that we live in the middle of it, haven't you?"

"In the middle of it?" Paula didn't know what to say. She felt a little stupid to be with the smartest person on the planet and to be just repeating the last words of his sentence, but she could not think of anything else she could do. She thought for a while until she realized "Of course!" she said. "We're part of an infinitely large room."

The star professor was impressed that Paula had understood the concept so quickly. "Come with me," he asked her. He led Paula up a corridor a long spiral staircase until they finally entered a large, dome-like room. Professor Prudens Astrum began to press a few buttons in front of a small screen, while Paula was still quite impressed by the room's size. Suddenly, a loud sound of metals banging on top of one another rang throughout the room, and its ceiling slowly began to open. Slowly, the light of the stars shone through the air, and Paula almost fainted when the stars suddenly approached her.

"Don't be frightened!", said the star professor, trying to calm her down. "The stars aren't really coming at us. If you look closely, you can see that the roof is made of glass; we are not in the open air. The dome is comparable to a giant telescope." He put a remote control of sorts in Paula's hand. "This controls what we see. If you press here, the field of view becomes larger, here, smaller. There you can move the image to the right, left, up, and down. If you want information about a planet or a star, bring it to the centre of the image and press here, which will display the data on - this - screen."

The more Paula changed the picture, the more she was impressed by the expansiveness of the space in which she lived. Paula became more and more familiar with the universe. For many stars, the star professor gave her a home and taught her everything she wanted to know. Since the professor was a wise man, he knew that his knowledge was limited, but the potential for more knowledge is *un*limited. He taught Paula that too, teaching her patience and modesty in a whimsical way.

Paula became an expert on the parts of the universe she could reach and explore with the technology available. Soon she knew not only the names and the distance of the planets around her own, but also their mass, composition, and all their individual peculiarities. Yet, the more she learned, the more she realized how little she did and could know in her life.

After half a moon she had heard everything the star professor knew about the universe. She would have liked to have stayed with him to look on and help him with his research, but she wanted to go home even more – especially considering the long time she had been away. The farewell was so difficult for her that she shed a few tears, but the professor's words brought a smile to her face. "I have given you the gift of knowledge. I hope you can share this gift with others."

Paula thought of Natalia and realized that knowledge behaved like love. It grew when you shared it.

When she left the professor's laboratory, she knew she had finally put an end to her search. She now knew what infinity meant and was just as sure she wanted to show it to others. She wanted to teach as the star professor, the love nymph, the spirit of the water, the number gnome, and even the fantastical Fantadu had. There was something to discover everywhere, and that was something she wanted the whole world to know.